FIRST WORDS

Jenny Tyler

Illustrated by Sue Stitt

Notes for Parents

This is a book for parents to share with their babies and toddlers. Each page has a clear picture of a familiar object which babies will learn to recognize and relate to real objects and, later, to name.

As they grow older, they will begin to take notice of the little pictures round the edges of the pages. These provide endless opportunities for parent and child to talk about the variety of objects which have the same name, the things that can be done with them and associated objects and events.

Conversations stimulated by looking at these pages will help very young children extend their language and understanding of the things around them.

At a later stage, but long before they learn to read, the words on each page will help children realize that sounds can be written down and that objects can be represented by both pictures and words.

With consultant advice from John Newson and Gillian Hartley of the Child Development Research Unit at Nottingham University, and Robyn Gee.

TOY WORDS

blocks

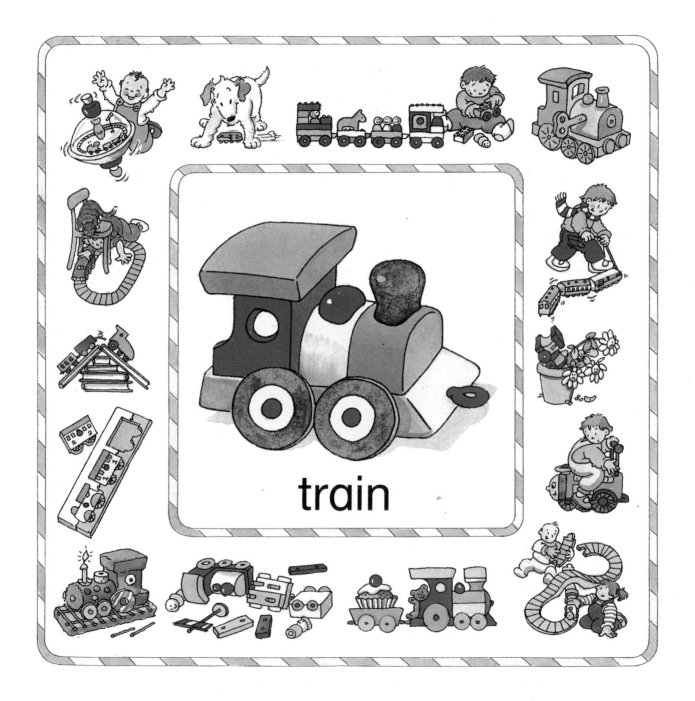

train

car

doll

tractor

airplane

ball

telephone

puzzle

balloon

telephone

train

ball

puzzle

balloon

doll

airplane

car

blocks

tractor

MEALTIME
WORDS

cookie

spoon

apple

bowl

ice cream

bib

cake

cup

egg

banana

apple

ice cream

cake

bib

spoon

egg

cup

bowl

cookie

banana

OUTDOOR WORDS

tree

leaf

flower

grass

mud

pond

rain

sun

snow

wind

pond

rain

tree

flower

wind

leaf

sun

mud

grass

snow

ANIMAL WORDS

cat

dog

COW

pig

sheep

horse

mouse

bird

rabbit

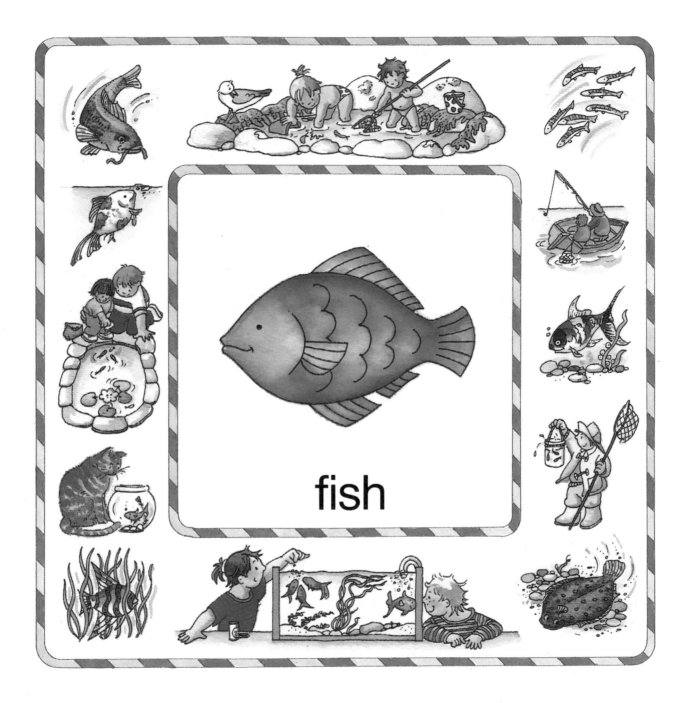

fish

cow

fish

horse

rabbit

cat

pig

mouse

bird

sheep

dog

SHOPPING WORDS

store

counter

bag

packet

scales

elevator

mirror

purse

cart

drink

counter

cart

elevator

packet

mirror

bag

drink

store

purse

scales

BEDTIME WORDS

bathtub

potty

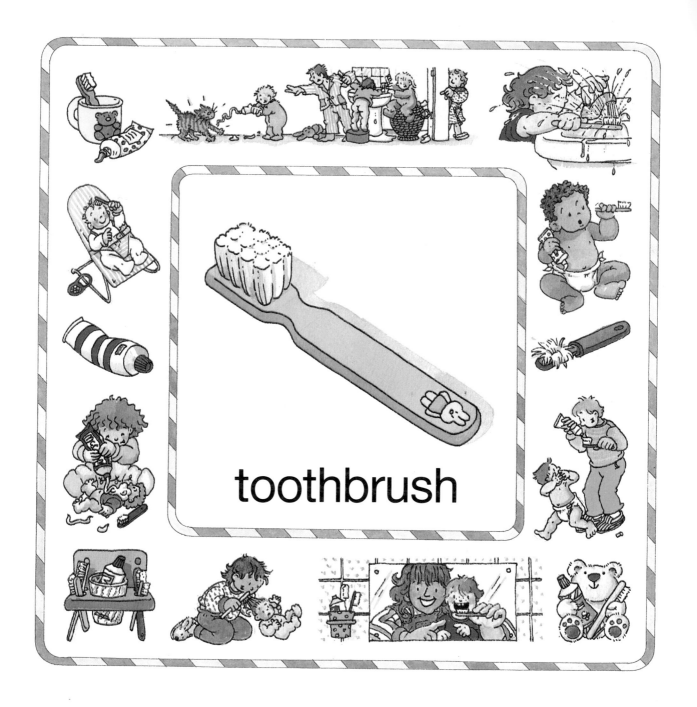

toothbrush

clock

teddy

book

stairs

curtains

bed

light

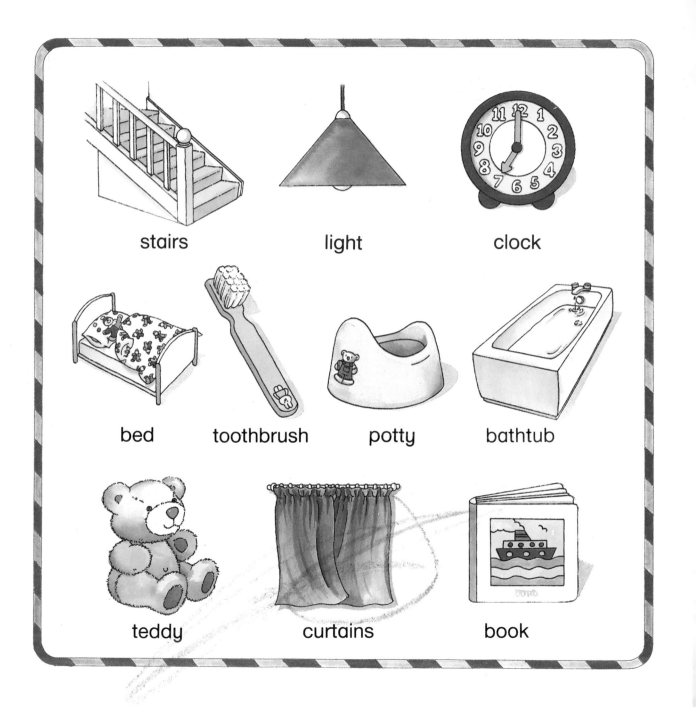

stairs

light

clock

bed

toothbrush

potty

bathtub

teddy

curtains

book

First published in 1989 by Usborne Publishing Ltd, Usborne House, 83-85 Saffron Hill, London EC1N 8RT.
Copyright © 1989 Usborne Publishing Ltd.